FOR: <u>DAD</u>

First published in the United States in 2023 by Crocodile Books
An imprint of Interlink Publishing Group, Inc.
46 Crosby Street
Northampton, Massachusetts 01060
www.interlinkbooks.com

Published simultaneously in the United Kingdom by HarperCollins *Children's Books*

Library of Congress Cataloging-in-Publication Data available.
ISBN 978-1-62371-722-3

Printed and bound by Vivar Printing in Malaysia

1 3 5 7 9 10 8 6 4 2

MUCH TOO BUSY

JOHN BOND

Pigeon is **extremely** busy.
Pigeon is doing **extremely** busy business things.

Rushing here.

Rushing there.

Pigeon was **SO** busy that he forgot
to look where he was going.

Pigeon was **SO** busy that before he knew it,
he didn't really know where he was at all.

Oh! I'm MUCH too BUSY for this, huffed Pigeon.

I absolutely do not have time for THIS.

Sitting on a log, staring into the distance, was Mouse.
Mouse was **definitely not** busy.

Mouse was just looking into the distance and wondering if that tree over there looked like an ice cream cone or a spaceship, when he spotted a **very** bothered-looking pigeon.

Can I help you?
asked Mouse.

YES! I'm **very, very busy** and I'm **very, very lost.**

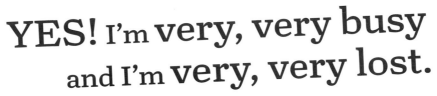

I have a **very** important thing to do and I need to be doing it **now.**

Oh dear, said Mouse. Perhaps I could help?

Yes, perhaps you could. But I'm **very busy.**
So if you could be quick about it.

Oh yes, of course,
said Mouse. Quick, quick. **Absolutely!**

So Mouse started to lead the way.

They hadn't been walking long when Mouse
stopped to investigate an interesting-looking leaf.

Ha! Pigeon, this leaf looks just like your foot.

No time for **that**, Mouse, huffed Pigeon.
Much too busy for that.

So they trudged

Soon Mouse came across a perfectly white feather.

Oh, **look**, Pigeon! It's a—

Just a feather, if you ask me, grumbled Pigeon.

No, no, absolutely not. We do not have time for feathers, Mouse.

But it looks just like a—

So on they we~~~~ ~~~~ed on.

As they came to a clearing, Mouse pointed excitedly up to the sky.
Well, Pigeon. Will you look at that!

That cloud looks
just like a DOG.

Nonsense, Mouse, said Pigeon. It's a cloud like any other cloud. Now can we please just **HURRY UP.**

So on they went . . .

Mouse all the time looking around him,

while Pigeon stared at his feet and thought about all the **very** important things he should be doing.

But the sky was growing dark,
and Mouse suddenly wasn't
quite so sure which way to go.

You're right, Pigeon, said Mouse.
This is **hopeless.**
I should have been looking where we were going
and not at all those silly things around me.

Pigeon stopped walking.

And for the first time he stopped thinking about all the things he should be doing.

He heard birds cheeping.

He heard the rustle of
leaves in the trees.

He heard his own thoughts.

And he heard Mouse . . .

No, no. That's **nonsense**, Mouse.

This is a **wonderful** forest.

Look at it all!

And look—can't you see—
that rock over there looks **just** like a **cat**!

Mouse looked. And it did.
The rock really did look
like a **cat**.

Oh yes, I **do see**, Pigeon!

So they both stopped and stared and admired
the funny-looking rock.

Do you know what else I see, Pigeon?

I can see the road—and your way home.

Oh, well.

That's nice, said Pigeon.

But let's just sit here for a little while and enjoy the forest, shall we?

And that's exactly what they did.